FOREHEAD FOREVER
A KISS THROUGH 201 QUOTES

FIROZ TATA

Copyright © Firoz Tata
All Rights Reserved.

ISBN 978-1-63957-808-5

This book has been published with all efforts taken to make the material error-free after the consent of the author. However, the author and the publisher do not assume and hereby disclaim any liability to any party for any loss, damage, or disruption caused by errors or omissions, whether such errors or omissions result from negligence, accident, or any other cause.

While every effort has been made to avoid any mistake or omission, this publication is being sold on the condition and understanding that neither the author nor the publishers or printers would be liable in any manner to any person by reason of any mistake or omission in this publication or for any action taken or omitted to be taken or advice rendered or accepted on the basis of this work. For any defect in printing or binding the publishers will be liable only to replace the defective copy by another copy of this work then available.

DEDICATING TO (YOU) WHO TAUGHT THE DUMB HEART WHAT LOVE IS BY PLANTING THE TRUE FEELINGS OF LOVE BREATHING EVEN AFTER LIFE.

LOVE YOU 'HEART' FOREVER.

LOVE IS CRUEL, YET ASTOUNDINGLY ETERNAL!

Contents

Preface   *vii*

Acknowledgements   *ix*

1. Quotes Cluster - A	1
2. Quotes Cluster - B	3
3. Quotes Cluster - C	6
4. Quotes Cluster - D	8
5. Quotes Cluster - E	10
6. Quotes Cluster - F	13
7. Quotes Cluster - G	15
8. Quotes Cluster - H	17
9. Quotes Cluster - I	20
10. Quotes Cluster - J	22
11. Quotes Cluster - K	24
12. Quotes Cluster - L	26
13. Quotes Cluster - M	28
14. Quotes Cluster - N	30
15. Quotes Cluster - O	32
16. Quotes Cluster - P	34
17. Quotes Cluster - Q	36
18. Quotes Cluster - R	38
19. Quotes Cluster - S	40
20. Quotes Cluster - T	42

Preface

Dear readers, it gives me endless pleasure and pride to present my third quote book 'Forehead Forever' in your hands. I am confident that this book too will serve its purpose in paving a long path in realising, spreading and understanding the beautiful feeling of true and innocent love among generations to come.

Once again, even this quote book is created by keeping in mind the portray of a very beautiful and extremely special individual who dwells in my mind, soul and heart. I would like to extend my genuine appreciation and life-long love to her for unknowingly inspiring me to visualise, conceive and birth best of the best of my creations in the form of poems and quotes. I worship her, and yes, she is my strongest inspiration from a far distance.

I have created more than 500 quotes and many of them are already published on **yourquotes.in**. Just like my first two quote books, 'The Connecting Hearts' and '16 June', even this book is the result of almost six months of scribbling and evolving the exact combination of vocabulary to build each quote. I have tried my level best not only to portray the feelings of love and beauty, but also the feelings of sadness, anger, hopes and determination through my various brainchild expressions.

I am confident that this publication will generate vigorous vibrations among my readers through the significant collection of my emotional and thought-provoking quotes. Those who find it difficult to articulate their emotions through words will feel encouraged to share my quotes with someone they deeply miss, care, admire, love, worship and are strongminded to have them in life.

PREFACE

The quotes in this book are purely creative thoughts based on my experiences, feelings and imagination. Any resemblance to other writings is completely unintentional and coincidental.

ppp

- The Author

Acknowledgements

From deep down my heart, I would like to express love and gratitude to my beloved mother Ms. Heera Tata and my loving rakhi sister Ms. Harshada Mhaske for always supporting me, my heart and my hard to fulfil wishes.

Without fail, I would love to extend my deepest appreciation and acknowledgement to a beautiful found and lost soul my readers will surely discover and feel again through my quotes that are delicately created by me in this heart-worming book.

- The Author

1
Quotes Cluster - A

Pampering her through a forehead kiss, waking up her with a cup of coffee, cooking her meals, making her feel like an Empress of your life, caring and appreciating her each day; every day, is the sexiest thing a man can ever offer in his relationship.
And sweetheart, these are more than my mere words!

❦❦❦

It takes hell of a strength to love and never ever be together, then to live together and never love.

❦❦❦

They look alike, but girl; there's a serious difference between your loving dogs and my determined wolves.

❦❦❦

Destiny was left with no other option but to face the dilemma of bending its ruthless rules to make them finally meet, always and forever.

❦❦❦

Hope is like a burnt wing bird that feels the dawn and carefully starts to sing again while it is still dark. The bird knows there is always the brightest sunrise waiting patiently on the other side of the darkest night horizon.
Hold on, never let go.

ppp

Using someone's emotions to fulfil your temporary selfishness is as hazardous as playing with fire.
Fire will surely provide the needed warmth, but don't tamper; it can prove fatal!

ppp

Obviously just one, he needed just one, but never found one; so he himself decided to be the one for himself.

ppp

Celebrating a festival may bring joy for a day, but celebrating the presence of your significant one daily makes entire life an exquisite carnival.
Appreciate your love before one day it gets depreciated.

ppp

She moves like a riddle riding through his mind and she has something that he fails to define. Can't deny the spark they caught from the start.
Tell him does he; does he have a final shot at her heart?

ppp

Occasionally the best medicine to suppress the pain is an atrocious aggressive approach towards conquering it.

ppp

# 2
Quotes Cluster - B

The most achingly complicated love story too can have a beautifully sad ending.
Hold on the hopes as the story never ends until we!

ಭಭಭ

Loving someone is an angelic fragrance smelled by the heart and not by the nostrils.

ಭಭಭ

It's hilarious to see your yesterday's so called 'supporter' as your today's 'jealous joker' in silence; changing it into tomorrow's just no one!

ಭಭಭ

She is an absolute astounding beauty not like those high heels super models. She is beautiful for the way she sees the world. She is beautiful for the way she ignites sparks in her brown sparkling eyes when she narrates something she madly loves.
She is beautiful for the ability to make others heal, even if her heart is fenced by doubts and darkness. No, she isn't

beautiful for something as temporary as her sensual looks. She is gracefully beautiful inside-out with her rare shining soul that belongs only to me, she fondly loves.

ϸϸϸ

Today's silent sacrifices can be your tomorrow's loudest triumph that no one ever expects.

ϸϸϸ

When a woman is cared, appreciated, respected and loyally loved the way she has always deserved, she becomes double 'your woman' she was ever before in life.
Her womanhood and love towards 'her man' multiplies million miles for million years.

ϸϸϸ

The moment she decided to break her golden shackles, they vowed to always and forever cuddle themselves in their own set rules; falling in bending rules of unconditional love.

ϸϸϸ

Falling in love with a person must be a beautiful experience, but falling in love with a soul is an expedition that lasts eternal as it's the only love that triumphs.

ϸϸϸ

None of us are perfect, but always pretend to be.
Only two imperfect people can lead perfect lives. Find love, not Mr/Ms perfection.

ϸϸϸ

When she transformed into a pretty purple butterfly, the caterpillars whispered not of her astounding beauty, but of her ravishing weirdness. They wanted to transform and restrict her back into what she always had been; forgetting she had strong wings eagerly awaiting to take her forever to the other side of the pleasant horizon.

ppp

3
Quotes Cluster - C

It took a million tears in rains to finally find you, yet you came exactly when you didn't need me!

ppp

The good in them for you today can be deadly treacherous for you tomorrow. It's all about the way you treat, deal, love and hate. The air can be felt, but not captured.

ppp

She never wanted a poisonous prince on a white horse from those fairy tales.
She needed a wolfy-warrior with a heart filled with pure warmth, fighting for his love-war with a fiery sword; resting her safely on his broad shoulders.

ppp

How much people may be unhappy in their married life, they fondly love to advice, "Please get married". How funny, how canny; are they jealous to see you happy?

ppp

A woman is a unique, picturesque, subtle flower who possesses several silent shades and aroma still certainly stung by societal honeybees. She holds several accounts of pain; reflecting clearly through her scared-shining eyes.

ᗪᗪᗪ

Loving wrong is worth than getting stabbed over and over by the right.
Wrong for one can be right for the other; just as one man's misfortune can be another's fortune.

ᗪᗪᗪ

It's easy to survive with a broken bone, then a broken heart! And the inconsiderate destinies departed them, may be to never meet again!

ᗪᗪᗪ

Love wasn't what you cultivated and kept claiming. It wasn't what you wished to hide and opted as secondary. It was what I kept on foolishly doing silently for decades until the day finally I whispered, "Goodbye Grace!"

ᗪᗪᗪ

A good loving woman is rare and hard to find; so sometimes a man has to snatch her from a careless crook who fails to value and appreciate what he fortunately has.

ᗪᗪᗪ

He is a man, man enough not to love a million girls as he loves to love only one in a million ways.
And that's for only you, my 'Heart'!

ᗪᗪᗪ

4
Quotes Cluster - D

When I won't reach you, my name will be enough; repeatedly to keep loving you passionately through my writings, for my peace.

ppp

An animal that leaps up with the injuries has licked its wounds silently for too long. Beware.

ppp

And since then she slept in his every invincible words that were specially designed only for the gorgeous her.

ppp

At first place you should be courageous enough to fall in love before you share your expert opinions and judgements about love to others. Have you?

ppp

It was the apex of his wholesome feelings that warmed his heart just once in life and soared forever mashing it to never return back and still he kept missing to be punished more and more as that was his first and last darling. He could never move on.

❧❧❧

Even a blunt needle is as good as a two edged sword to stab a good soul and limpid heart. However, little less painful than living amongst those who hardly attempts to know you; understand you.

❧❧❧

Used lips for terrifying truth, voice for killer kindness, ears for classic compassion, hands for Christ's children and unhealed heart for loyal love to those who miserably failed to love her back.

❧❧❧

She propels through the power of prayer to prolong and that's her utmost elegance that finally forced him to fall in her silhouette's love.

❧❧❧

The dumb devil whispered in my ear how I knew my way around the haunting halls of the hell. I replied: "I did not need a map, for the deadly darkness was my lone loyal friend. I am the endless end of my friend".

❧❧❧

Finally, that was the only feeling of love accountable for his loving heart to be scared of that special woman as he never wanted to lose her. A good man scares only from two things: The God he bows and a woman he deeply devotes.

❧❧❧

5
Quotes Cluster - E

What made grace looked more graceful wasn't her splendour, appearance or what she attained, but her oceanic love and audacity to trust. No matter the dusk around her soul; that brightest ray of hope ran wild within her core, and that was the only way she once again came alive, showing up in everything until now.

ᗞᗞᗞ

Don't love me for what I am.
Love me as your heart passionately compelled you to.

ᗞᗞᗞ

It's an ongoing unbreakable and invisible connection with an individual that the soul picks up again and again irrespective of time and endless space over a lifetime. Simply gravitated to that one person at the soul level not because it's our rare unique compliment, but because by being with that soul we are somehow heightened with a thrust to become whole forever.

ᗞᗞᗞ

If I could be any part of you, I would be that drop of your sweet tear that conceives in your bruised heart, borns in your brown eyes, pants on your blushing cheeks and finally perishes on your luscious lips.

ppp

Love prevails only where respect resides. Claiming love without respect is just like riding a bicycle without wheels! No respect! No love!

ppp

She knew with whom she was dancing within in her mind espousing to see the good in his everything. Her energetic elegance could birth out the best in the delighted devil.

ppp

Read me as much as you like, but you won't know me for I differ in hundred shades of black from what you see me to be. Put yourself behind my eyes and see me as I see myself for I have chosen to finally dwell alone in a place only someone special can see, and not any beautiful witch!

ppp

Don't treat them the way they treat you. Treat them the way they are forced to treat you the way you and they both deserve to be treated by each another with oceans of love.

ppp

During the wheel of our life cycle we can cheat as many people as we can, but will miserably fail to cheat our own heart. Sweetheart, the heart knows it all.

ppp

FOREHEAD FOREVER

There is a man out there longing to give you everything that you are giving to a man who isn't man enough to accept and appreciate it. Don't be a woman that needs a man and accepts his ruthless rejections.

Be a woman a man needs for his role-recognition.

ϷϷϷ

6
Quotes Cluster - F

You just miserably misunderstand the taste of that fire until it kisses you at least once in life.
Never play with someone's innocent feelings.

▷▷▷

Childhood, youth, skin, scars, soul, self-respect, dignity and bones too. And then comes the turn of a fragile heart.
Their silent share of sufferings, thanking beautiful life.

▷▷▷

Immense patience and intense efforts are the tests to prove that you once loved, you still love and will always keep loving. Stay firm, never let go!

▷▷▷

It wasn't the enchanting beauty of astounding her that caught my eyes, but her million scars on heart that forced me to fall in love with her heavenly soul, eternally.

▷▷▷

Nothing makes you more beautiful than your own belief that you are already inside-out beautiful.

🍂🍂🍂

And it was only the time who could narrate if he succeeded to handover his heart to someone else or if she could blush for someone else.

🍂🍂🍂

The worst darkness is the sadness that is worthless to be said as sadness resulting in your heartfelt lifelong solace.

🍂🍂🍂

Today's childhood will be tomorrow's manhood only if fathers first educate their fatherhood.

🍂🍂🍂

A zillion stars twinkling in the night sky of intense faith and hopes. A trillion memories of that hearty-hope-image. Her black and white snap causing vivacious vibrations and wracking waves into my heart that was already lit on fire.

🍂🍂🍂

Natural silver tranquillity, masked white wildness, enchanting brown eyes, blushing red cheeks, wine-sweet lips and the sexiest simplicity at its highest peak is the rare beauty she possessed.

🍂🍂🍂

7
Quotes Cluster - G

You just don't need to be physically together with the person you deeply love. Adding them into your daily prayers is the purest form that they are invisibly present with you residing deep down in your core.

ppp

A genuine gentleman gets unstoppable from falling in love with that valorous warrior who sculpts herself from her own brokenness and ashes. A silent lover of strength and substance, not status and society.

ppp

Genuine chivalry towards woman is the first step entering the door of her hurricane heart.

ppp

The minute she timidly spoke to him,
he bravely started to fall in her love, the same way he felt asleep slowly, then just all at once.

ppp

And then after she refused to endure more, she transformed from bliss to blaze!

ᗏᗏᗏ

A strong woman knows she has strength enough for that heartless journey, but a woman of strength knows that exact once-in-a-lifetime journey-jump where she'll alter into her strongest form for all her remaining breaths.

ᗏᗏᗏ

The quench of a real love is achieved after sleeping in the pit of a final straight line, perhaps.

ᗏᗏᗏ

You presume they'll portray you 'weak' as you too have a heart that cries through eyes. Let's educate them. "There is nothing stronger than a man who isn't afraid to taste his tears and even powerful is he who isn't shy to show them rolling down his cheeks.

ᗏᗏᗏ

Cooking for a loved one shouldn't be a heartless formality, but a daily dose of passionate desire for the loved one's palates and plate. Flourish unconditional love through cooking, not through formal self-chocking!

ᗏᗏᗏ

You can travel around the globe, sojourn various states; return back home and feel, home sweet home, but there can never be the sweetest home fortified firmly in the heart of a special festive woman. A temple for forever devotion.

ᗏᗏᗏ

8
Quotes Cluster - H

It's better to love and to be loved in a million mile distant absent than to be unloved and hidden-hated in a meaningless proximity presence. Pure connections conceive amongst silent words and grows forever in solace.

♥♥♥

Like a crafty thief at night armed with his pretty lies he'll haunt you, consume you! You can't let him win. His fear be your friend guiding you, fulfilling you, keep loving you!

♥♥♥

Selflessly donating that sustained your body all life is the best possible way to live life after death in else's body.

♥♥♥

Upbringing of a child is much more uplifting among loving people without blood relations.
Growing among unhappy parents make them learn to accept compromise and sorrow.

♥♥♥

We fail, keep failing, keep miserably failing, just can't stop from failing, each effort keeps failing, will fail and will fail forever to reject, forget, refuse or not accept that you love me and I too deeply, but fail to avoid or refuse loving. Simply two lives' failure to stop loving each other madly and silently.

ppp

My woman's eyes are the shining mirror of her soul reflecting everything that seems to be hidden in the blankets of agony; and like a silver-shine mirror they reflect the soul looking into them.

ppp

Her deceptive beauty can be seen through face, skin, clothes, shoes and makeup she wears, but never perishing beauty is only discovered through eyes, language, thoughts and her tender heart that pounds just for the one. His gifted grace to him.

ppp

Her beauty was deceiving, deceptive and dangerous; but his intelligence was minacious, menacing and murderous to never fall in trap.

ppp

The powerful work of my love began only after falling in the pain and later with the person.
True love is never fetched that easy.

ppp

If I get out alive from this, not we; as I know you have to and will for me. Someday, someway, somewhere, somehow

I'll find you and say, "I may not be your first date, first kiss or even your first marriage, but surely I'll be your first love and last everything. Can't stop loving you, 'Heart'.

༄༄༄

9
Quotes Cluster - I

He doesn't follow where she goes, but if she makes an abrupt turn, he'll be there to hold her from falling. A man who's such a rock be lighter than the air, wider than an ocean and deeper than an abyss.

♡♡♡

Patiently waiting is the strongest silent way to say, "I used to, will and keep loving you forever".

♡♡♡

Just as a broken wing bird can never fly high, a scared hearted coward can never fall in love.

♡♡♡

They say nothing comes free in life, but the best thing you drench is the celestial shining love without efforts, undeniably lasting longer.
A remedy, if fortunate; covered in disguise.

♡♡♡

Byes and goodbyes are ridiculous myths for those who love each other silently, madly and deeply but refuse to agree, accept and say. Time in some way brings them together as universe too favours them.
There stands no chance for silly byes and goodbyes between such two inseparable people.

ppp

And perhaps...
It was not the hardest part to break the news to already broken heart.

ppp

You said move on. The stubborn I said never. My love, those were the two hanging hearts on invisible string that were only meant to be together, always and forever.

ppp

None of the honesty is as comparable and is unmatchable than seen in the never tiring eyes of a mother holding her ever loving child.

ppp

A wise skeleton said to the other, "Buddy it's better to die single without a drop of water on your deathbed, than marrying a shit, suffocating all life."

ppp

A hunter that loves not only knows to hunt his dangerous prey, but also knows to rescue the pretty victim from the claws of the predator.

ppp

10
Quotes Cluster - J

She was his manipulating game for marriage,
but another man's triumphed treasure.

▷▷▷

At the bottom of the bucket list was the only sin he would madly love to commit by stealing her from herself, her people; once again igniting their never ceasing hopes.

▷▷▷

Love was just a small word until she came riding out of the dark giving it a colossal meaning, but just once.

▷▷▷

When mysterious mind accepted, the persistent heart simply rejected to accept to let her go.

▷▷▷

Someone disappearing abruptly from life doesn't affect your worth, but reflects their priorities.

▷▷▷

Do what you think is best for you,
I'll do what I think is best for us, and that's called, 'love'.

ppp

Your parenting only succeeds when your boy becomes a man gently tough enough to kindly treat someone's daughter righteous and with utmost chivalry; loving her just as he loves his every breath, never razing her mentally and physically.

ppp

The worst mistake of a good woman is to keep tolerating an absurd man and assume all men are the same; weeping quietly. Move on.

ppp

Man's emptiness is when he is surrounded by many noisy vessels, but he fails and refuses to make noise like them, giving birth to his beautiful uniqueness.

ppp

Sleeping and walking alone in rains has a common benefit.
No one can see those precious diamonds rolling down.
A peace finally followed by pieces of an innocent heart.

ppp

11
Quotes Cluster - K

The she who doesn't ask for anything, deserves everything. Treat her well or burn in hell.

♡♡♡

It's a divine bell to be loved by an unexpected one, but it can't be more heavenly to reciprocate the same with respect and loyalty.

♡♡♡

He practices over you when he praises your beauty through his web of words.
Just as a butterfly loves nectar, rat loves cheese; he adores only the beauty of his woman, oh! yes please.

♡♡♡

Life is like a first kiss. You never know how long it's going to last. Be grateful for negatives, as they strengthen our character as a person.

♡♡♡

Care is selfless until you express it, affection is pointless until you show it and using someone's innocent feelings is worthless and has adverse consequences.

▷▷▷

And perhaps....
Just wasn't there anyone like her, which hasn't been a fluke; but his meaningful miracle!

▷▷▷

Have you ever felt that rare strength love infuses inside your silent soul in a bruised and broken body? Think!

▷▷▷

Bruises on the body can be healed, but childhood scars on soul can never be.

▷▷▷

Take every chance in what you firmly believe in, or repent later after opportunity vanishes.

▷▷▷

He was raised as a tame caged animal who learnt to write his mind on paper, stitching his lips forever.

▷▷▷

12
Quotes Cluster - L

Trust it. Time is a remedy wrapped in disguise.

♡♡♡

Your soul never falls in love to leave, but your heart does live long enough hoping to never fall out of it.

♡♡♡

A lady without beautiful morning smile, is a bright day without sunshine.

♡♡♡

And then writing became a colourful curse making so easy for the fingers to happily bleed for an unhealed heart; then, now and forever.

♡♡♡

Though they kept getting old with every tick of time, the nights refused to; and remained young until they met one day, multiplying million memories mentally.

♡♡♡

A few songs and a few rarely beautiful memories are the worst nemesis of a person during heartache that has to be relished without choice.

ᗞᗞᗞ

Your mother is a bond through blood, bones and flesh and not through materialistic web taking care of your child like a nanny. Less valuing leads to more losing.

ᗞᗞᗞ

The worst loss of a moron man is to lose a good woman who appears racing rare and disappears at once. Treasure her!

ᗞᗞᗞ

Loving so right at such a wrong time is an unforgiving fight that he faced until his final sunsets at the life's horizon.

ᗞᗞᗞ

Mental, physical and the pains of a mistreated bruised heart are bottles of finest life-bitter-wines, but the daily dose of agony due to gradual change deep down inside your larger than life silent significant due to their hurtful surroundings are the bitterest life-lethal-acids to gulp.

ᗞᗞᗞ

13
Quotes Cluster - M

It wasn't pumping in me to play, but you did for which I paid a lifelong price. That wasn't your second toy, but only my dumb heart who fell for you so strongly.

ᗞᗞᗞ

He worshipped his Goddess more than anyone, never knowing she was simply a selfish human who was only craving for self-love, not love; making him never falling in love ever again.

ᗞᗞᗞ

A fortunate 'He' evolves into more of a man when he decides to choose sentiments above semen by stepping up to the plate another man has heartlessly left on the table.

ᗞᗞᗞ

A woman holds deeper dark secrets than an undiscovered ocean! Love her, care her, value her to learn her.

ᗞᗞᗞ

It's only the scorching resolve of love that keeps bringing you back again and again to finally pull over the impossible.

༙༙༙

Lesser you react to every situation, every word; more you attract peace and distant from negative overthinking.

༙༙༙

The best yet crazy part of me is, I love to love even the wrecking wrong. The worst part of me is I hate not to strike hard and fast when a set line is crossed and I am done with their nasty behaviour!

༙༙༙

The happiest thing was to get support and love from unexpected ones when I was down and out of work and life. The saddest thing is they dropped their courtesy like clothes, deciding to turn their faces from my rising Sun!

༙༙༙

I am a wizard through words who use praise as a toilet paper and criticism as yet another step to climb the ladder to reach what is meant to be mesmerised as mine, and I'll.

༙༙༙

Her velvety lips deserved and were destined for the sedation he may have provided and not the sedation she received from the glass she surely started to love more than him. Sad, very sad!

༙༙༙

14
Quotes Cluster - N

It's not a fight, but a war that'll destroy either one or both. Though I will win, but end up being a loser; vice versa. No problem it's a raging fire that our hearts have set-up.

▷▷▷

The only similarity between you and me is that we both were surrounded in blazing fires, I would save you and you too would save yourself! Still I smiled because that's what I deserved for loving the wrong larger than my own life.

▷▷▷

Messing with the first feelings of an innocent heart is like writing an end of your own destiny sooner or later, with your own two hands.

▷▷▷

A single unknown enemy is more treacherous than an entire troupe of army standing a few metres away. Beware of the known, unknown!

▷▷▷

Underestimating or neglecting the determined silence is as good as turning face from first fire spark in dry woods, thinking won't catch deadly fire.

ᖘᖘᖘ

The worst mistake of an oversmart fool is to love arguing and not learning.

ᖘᖘᖘ

Certain tales do not end that easy.
They have to be paused for time; though they remain to be continued, just like yours and mine!

ᖘᖘᖘ

Once loved is forever loved; or was never loved.

ᖘᖘᖘ

They were very same with two very different destinies longing to meet at some point; just as an ocean at its horizon who seems to kiss the sky, but unfortunately can't.

ᖘᖘᖘ

A writer: He was done fighting as a child, picking up a pen to keep kissing the papers for the rest of his life.

ᖘᖘᖘ

15

Quotes Cluster - O

It be so beautiful if every heart was touched to heal and cared only to love; just once and then never; forever.

▷▷▷

If I said I miss you madly. Would you believe?
Please don't, it's an utter lie.

▷▷▷

How long can you ride your life by keeping others pleased and satisfied at the cost of your peace and happiness?
It's soul damaging.

▷▷▷

The agony of chest-stabbing is much more painful than the agony of back-stabbing; as you know the face who simply loved to stab. Wow! Thanks.

▷▷▷

The biggest dare is self-belief and you better trust that.

▷▷▷

Healing was just not possible when your page refused to turn, and thus, this wasn't how our tale was supposed to meet its end. And I swear.

ᚦᚦᚦ

Although she wasn't true to herself, but always true to him, and perhaps that was the last best thing that could ever happen to him!

ᚦᚦᚦ

I'll dismantle you in the most graceful way possible. When I am done ruining your soul; you will finally understand why storms are named after people.
Won't let forget the name of the fiend, which is me.

ᚦᚦᚦ

Underestimating you is the best blunder they can make. Let them; wait, watch, grow and end!

ᚦᚦᚦ

Be a gentleman through achieved heart and not through ascribed birth.

ᚦᚦᚦ

16
Quotes Cluster - P

One day you puncture your own heart with your own hands so it never throbs for that air which was the freshest of all. It did what it had to do, keeping the painful principles ahead of love.

ppp

And so you see, it's hard to love wrong, harder to hate the right and hardest to stay hurt; hanging the heart by an invisible thread.

ppp

Don't do what they say to do.
Do what they never want you to definitely do.
Do what's best only for you.

ppp

And then when she decided to select her unbearable likings over his years of pure first love and dedication; he sadly refused her, stabbing his own heart.

ppp

They wanted every single piece of her.
He merely needed an ounce of her sexiest heart, which wasn't much.

▷▷▷

It's a beautiful dream to love and never be together than to live together without loving each other.

▷▷▷

Mastering, moulding and merging the words for a beautiful creation is as challenging as making someone else's unhappy wife officially yours; forever. However, both attainable with patience, passion and purity.
Don't let others write your story.

▷▷▷

A person that refuses to escape your mind is the hostage that refuses to leave your hurricane heart.

▷▷▷

Love isn't quitting your own set standards low for the selfish satisfaction of other.

▷▷▷

Investing energy and time in those who are ready to do the same in return is not rudeness, but smartness.

▷▷▷

17
Quotes Cluster - Q

Correcting a fool leads you to frowning hate.
Correcting a wise earns you an adorable appreciation.
Be smart before correcting.

ppp

A single moment of hate devastates a lifetime of work, whereas a single moment of loyal love can break barriers that takes a lifetime to build.
Hate embraced everywhere, love almost nowhere!

ppp

Seas aren't crossed by merely staring waters, so as our life without hard work and resolve.

ppp

He who deeply loves never snatches for personal gains. He who hardly or do not, doesn't returns what snatched, knowingly or unknowingly.

ppp

Interpreting silence as weakness can just be the beginning of silent retaliation.

༄༄༄

A general human tendency:
The more you keep yourself available, the more they ignore and avoid you.
The more you ignore, the more you get attention by them. How's that?

༄༄༄

Your biggest success to succeed for what you desperately dream is succeeded only by controlling your lineal line of boiling blood.
Check aggression, capture destination.

༄༄༄

Just as salt doesn't take time to absorb moisture, sensitive people do not take much time to get hurt.
Choose your actions and words wisely!

༄༄༄

Being his long life experimental goat is your choice.
So chose witty or die pity.

༄༄༄

Sometimes the weight of a sin is less than the strength of loving the wrong so very right!

༄༄༄

18
Quotes Cluster - R

The heart that keeps crying, finally creates colours through its writings! Love you, 'Purple'.

♡♡♡

Sometimes being lifelong single is a choice, until your soul connects with the correct one.

♡♡♡

The moment you decide to kiss your tears and taste them, a new electrifying version of you conceives and births. Stay determined!

♡♡♡

As soon as you realise depleting of your worth from them, distant immediately!

♡♡♡

Besides self, let no one ever know the degree of determination you can and have already reached.

♡♡♡

And perhaps...
Sometimes being physically present is far better than financial assistance.

🙵🙵🙵

There is a difference between being delusion and having a death wish!

🙵🙵🙵

People receive more flowers on their graves than in hands during their lifetime.
Appreciate and value first those who are still alive.

🙵🙵🙵

My angel side still can't stop loving you foolishly and surely will only keep longing for you forever more than my one in life, but my devil side says that your destruction is written by my claws. Can't help, as someone has to win.
Your angel or my devil?

🙵🙵🙵

He is a master of true love and loyalty, but his black vile side is doctorate of hailstorm hate if you mess with his unhealed heart.

🙵🙵🙵

19

Quotes Cluster - S

Sometimes too late to think and sometimes never too late to rethink to start again with a massive change.

ᗡᗡᗡ

She gracefully rampaged and ate his heart piece by piece until it stopped forever. Don't act in love, just fall in love.

ᗡᗡᗡ

A raging storm never knocks the door to step in. It blows up everything to enter your double-face life. And so do I!

ᗡᗡᗡ

I'll forgive you if you hurt me, but I'll hurt you if you use me by becoming the author of your poisonous pain.

ᗡᗡᗡ

The practice to ignore for a while and return wagging tail in selfish expectation is the habit of a dog. Oh! No much difference? Happy barking, people!

ᗡᗡᗡ

The best strategy to stay in and at peace is to be a well-mannered savage and sweetly subtract them from life; torturing your innocent mind, heart and soul.

ppp

A lifelong gift you bestowed on me is the pleasure that ends with either end, eternally.

ppp

Sharing your secrets with a stranger can make you fall in love for his super sweetness.
Hey! Be watchful; today's best pal can be tomorrow's worst foe if you try to deceive!

ppp

And perhaps...
Pure love is like a strawberry wine that is left with no other option but to get sweeter and sweeter with the passage of time, multiplying into decades.

ppp

It would be a great all life battle to have at least an ounce of her than the venomous love his soul had to gulp; insensitively now loving her through heart; eternally.

ppp

20
Quotes Cluster - T

Marry when your soul finally falls for;
neither your heart nor the demanding age.

ppp

Just as no other person can sense your shoe-bite, no one
can feel the gravity of your heartache.
Enjoy lonely! Perish silently!

ppp

Death is an ultimate sweet destiny of life that rides
speedily towards its end.

ppp

A 'Tata' is a Tata through a brainy brain breathing within
the heart and not by ascribed second name 'Tata'.

ppp

Dear darling, only our determination can create an
unexpected love story that we had always hoped to write.

ppp

Sometimes stop seeing good in them, and start observing what they don't wish to reveal.
None are one-line story.

ppp

She was swept away by his charm making him drown in her exquisite beauty, both falling for each other and then falling apart eternally!

ppp

It's only the bursting up of dormant determination that will ignite my last candle in this dark deep abyss; welcoming a year of now or never.
Stay focused. Stay strong.

ppp

You wanted her to be your passionate power, but little you were aware she was your purple sugary poison loving you for the rest of your life.

ppp

Waiting and waiting and once again waiting is a strong sign of your tireless broken heart who fondly loves something and especially someone.
It's a rare strength. Hold on, never let it go!

ppp

Today's creation will be my tomorrow's history in your hands, after I leave for the stars to never come back.
Love you 'HEART'. Cya AGAIN!

ppp

www.ingramcontent.com/pod-product-compliance
Lightning Source LLC
LaVergne TN
LVHW021739060526
838200LV00052B/3364